This Little Tiger book
belongs to:

_____

_____

_____

For Ailsa and Lyndall – B D

For Jammy and Esme – J P

LITTLE TIGER PRESS LTD,
an imprint of the Little Tiger Group
1 Coda Studios, 189 Munster Road, London SW6 6AW
www.littletiger.co.uk

First published in Great Britain 2020
This edition published 2021

Text by Becky Davies
Illustrations by Jennie Poh
Text and illustrations copyright © Little Tiger Press 2020

Printed in China • LTP/2800/3503/1020

2 4 6 8 10 9 7 5 3 1

The Forest Stewardship Council® (FSC®) is an international,
non-governmental organisation dedicated to promoting responsible
management of the world's forests. FSC® operates a system of forest
certification and product labelling that allows consumers to identify
wood and wood-based products from well-managed forests.

For more information about the FSC®, please visit their website at www.fsc.org

FSC
www.fsc.org
MIX
Paper from
responsible sources
FSC® C017606

Little Turtle
and the Sea

Becky Davies

Jennie Poh

LITTLE TIGER
LONDON

It began with a thunder storm.

Ψ   The rain lashed and the waves crashed as Little Turtle pushed her way out of the nest, and onto the sodden sand.

She needed to be quick. One flipper in
front of the other, she pulled herself down
the beach towards the sea, and safety.

Thunder rumbled in the sky as Little Turtle slipped into the sea for the very first time. The water rose to meet her and she was tossed and turned in the spray.

Which way was up? Tiny turtles splashed all around her, calling, "Swim, swim!"

Just when Little Turtle's flippers were tiring,
she managed to hitch a ride.

Her journey had begun!

Warm currents carried
Little Turtle over a carpet
of colour.

She danced with the swaying
seagrass. She swam with fish of
every shape and size.

"What beauty!" she said.
Happy and content, Little Turtle
climbed into a cosy cave and
slept.

Months passed, and Turtle
was no longer little.

She had outgrown her
hidey-hole . . .

. . . but she would never outgrow the ocean.
Turtle swam onwards through mile after
mile of dazzling open water.

She was quite alone, and yet she didn't
feel lonely. The ocean was her friend.

At last, Turtle's journey was complete. She had
made it to the other side of the world.

"Home," sighed Turtle.

And what a home it was!

Foraging and feeding, Turtle lived there happily
for many years.

Until one day, it was time for her to return . . .

Turtle swam across the ocean, back to the beach where she had been born.

She made this journey many times, but found that the same journey was always different.

Turtle, too, was different. As she grew each year, her love for the ocean grew with her.

She saw new sights, made new
friends and welcomed some
new little turtles into the world.

Then one day, the ocean itself was different.

Colours disappeared, and Turtle found strange new creatures swimming beside her.

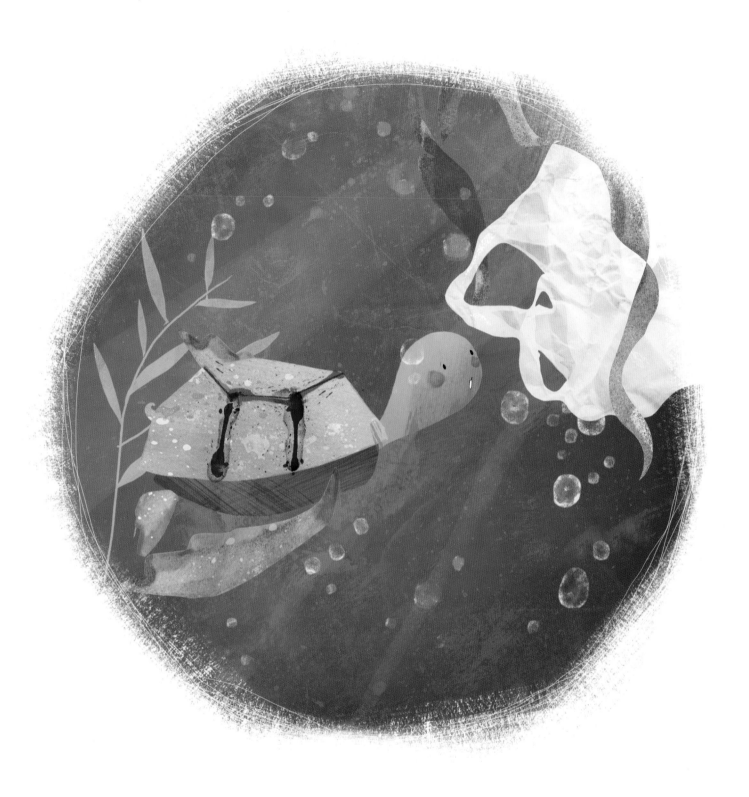

"Friend?" she asked. But she was met with silence.

The strangeness
grew and grew.

And Turtle felt lost in the
places she knew most.

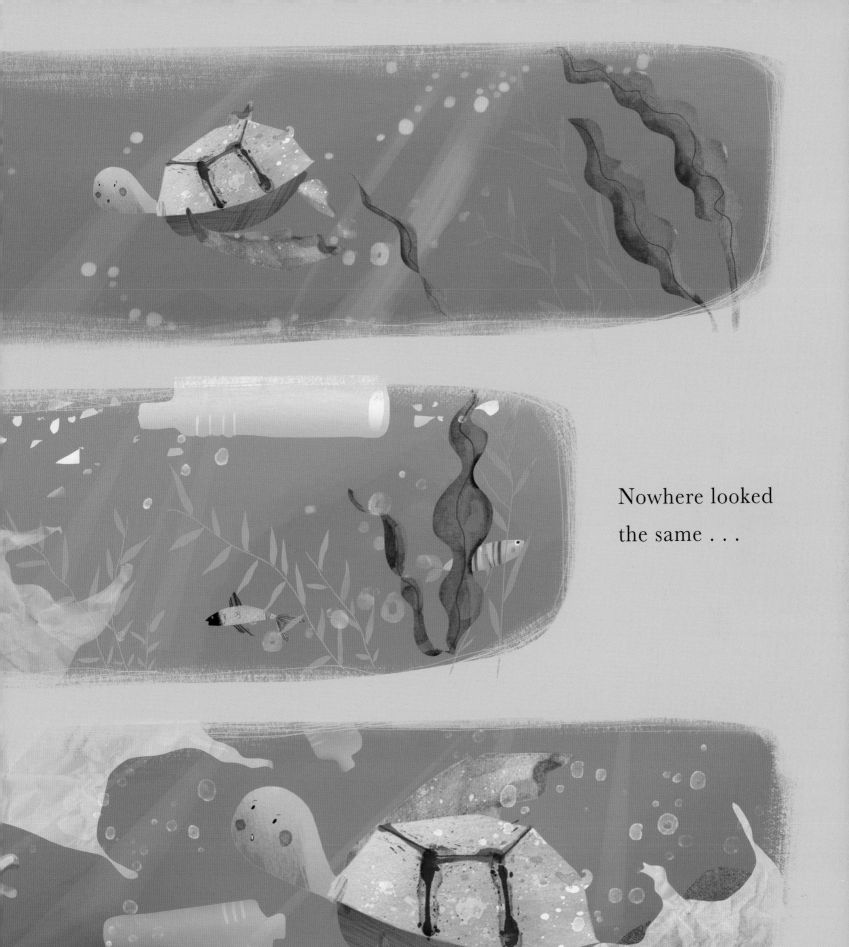

Nowhere looked
the same . . .

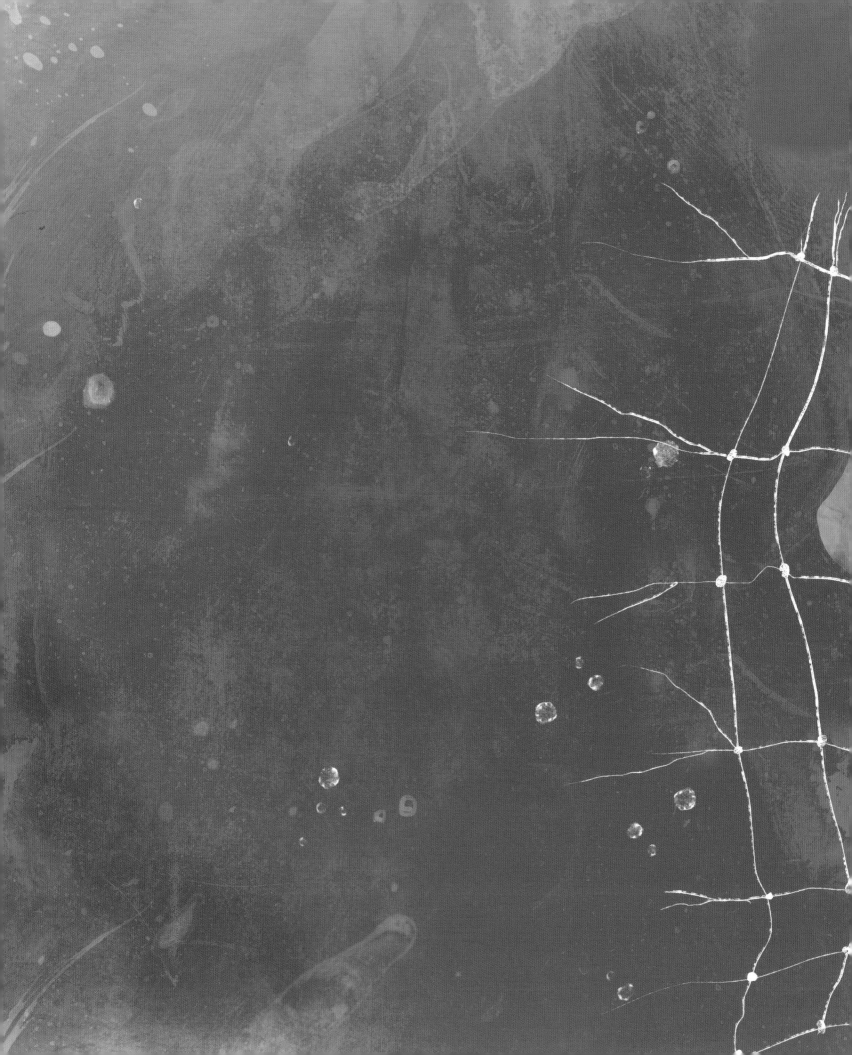

The ocean no longer felt like a friend.

"Hello?" she spoke into the darkness.

But Turtle was alone.

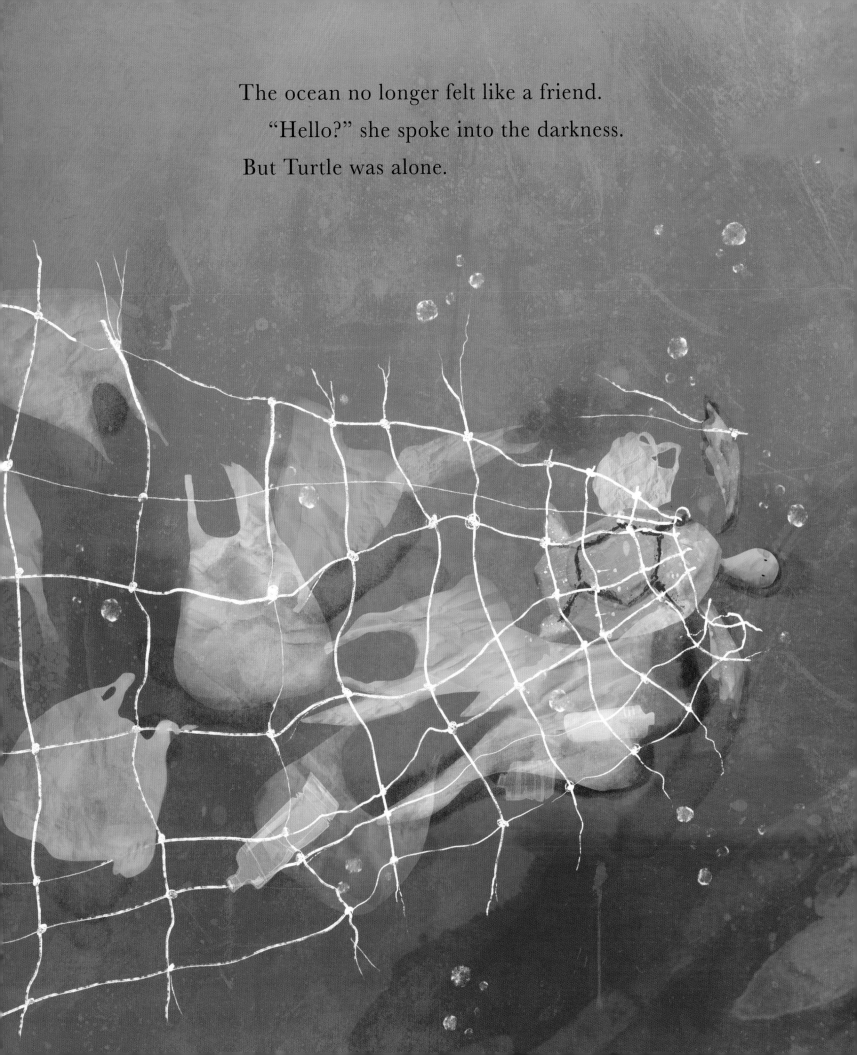

Just when Turtle thought
her journey was over forever,
figures emerged from the
strangeness and swam
towards her.

Turtle was freed!

Little by little, she watched as they tended the seagrass, the coral, and her friends.

"Thank you," she said. They had returned her to the ocean . . .

. . . and began to return Turtle's ocean to her.
It was beautiful once more, and she loved it
with her whole heart.

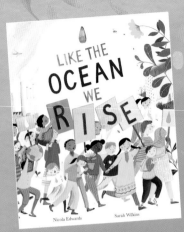

LIKE THE
OCEAN
WE
RISE

Nicola Edwards   Sarah Wilkins

Dear
Earth

Isabel Otter   Clara Anganuzzi

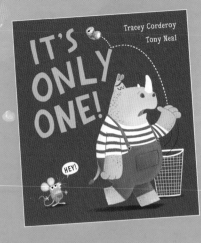

Tracey Corderoy
Tony Neal

IT'S
ONLY
ONE!

HEY!

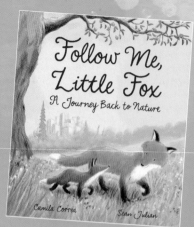

Follow Me,
Little Fox
A Journey Back to Nature

Camila Correa   Sean Julian

Inspire a love for our planet with these nurturing books from Little Tiger.

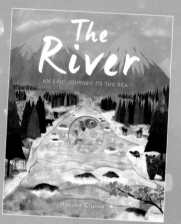

The
River

AN EPIC JOURNEY TO THE SEA

Hanako Clulow

A world beneath the waves

SEA

Britta Teckentrup

LiTTLE TiGER

For information regarding any of the above titles or for our
catalogue, please contact us: Little Tiger Press Ltd, 1 Coda Studios,
189 Munster Road, London SW6 6AW • Tel: 020 7385 6333
E-mail: contact@littletiger.co.uk • www.littletiger.co.uk